Sometimes
I feel...

Dedicated to my mother, Georgina, without whom
this book wouldn't exist. Also to my father, Stephen, my sister,
Louisa, and my husband, Tom, for their endless support.

BIG PICTURE PRESS

This edition published in the UK in 2021 by Big Picture Press.
First published in the UK in 2020 by Big Picture Press
an imprint of Bonnier Books UK,
The Plaza, 535 King's Road, London, SW10 0SZ
Owned by Bonnier Books
Sveavägen 56, Stockholm, Sweden
www.templarco.co.uk/big-picture-press
www.bonnierbooks.co.uk

1 3 5 7 9 10 8 6 4 2

ISBN 978-1-78741-726-7

This book was typeset in Cabrito Didone
The illustrations were created with watercolour
and ink and finished digitally

Edited by Carly Blake
Designed by Olivia Cook & Marty Cleary
Production by Neil Randles

Printed in China

Sarah Maycock

Sometimes I feel...

BPP

Sometimes

I feel as

BIG

as a

Bear.

But there will always
be someone bigger
than me and sometimes
I will feel small.

Sometimes
I feel as
HAPPY
as a
Lark.

But not all days can be filled with song . . .

. . . and sometimes I will need time
before I can join in with the chorus.

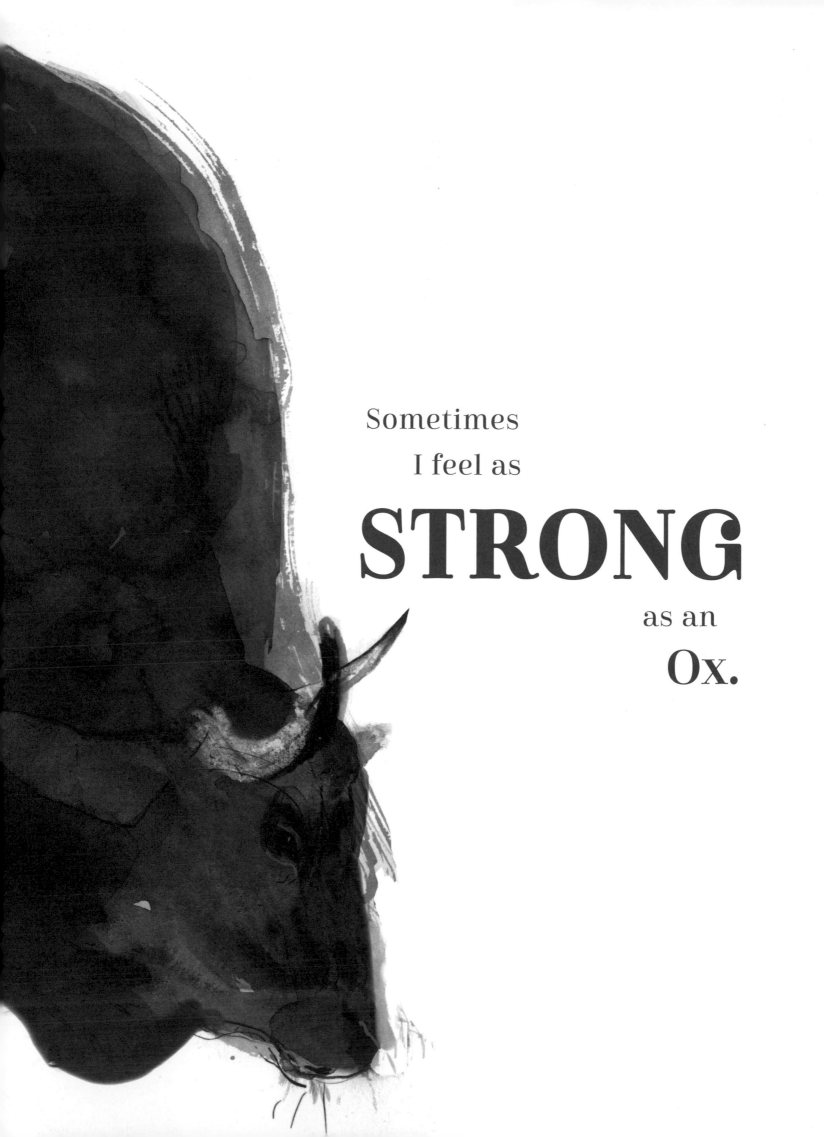

Sometimes
I feel as

STRONG

as an

Ox.

But the days that leave me
worn out and weary
will make me stronger tomorrow.

Sometimes
I feel as

BUSY

as a
Bee.

But slowing down to see the beauty all around me is time just as well spent.

Sometimes

I feel as

BRAVE

as a

Lion.

But when the roar of the storm
seems frightening . . .

. . . I know it will pass
and so will my fear.

Sometimes
I feel as
CUNNING
as a
Fox.

But when I'm too clever
for my own good,
I get caught out.

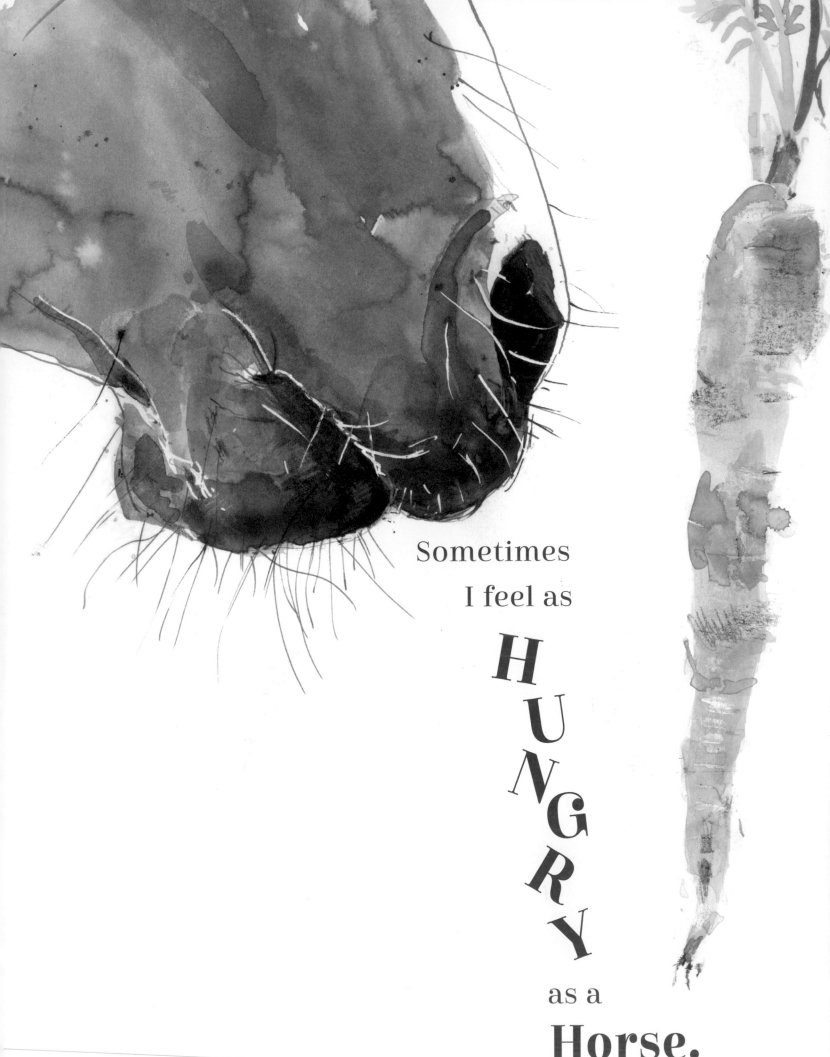

Sometimes
I feel as

HUNGRY

as a

Horse.

But stopping when
I've had enough . . .

. . . means there's plenty left
for everyone else.

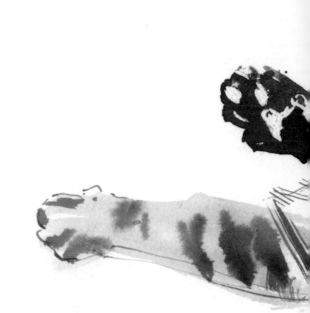

Sometimes

I feel as

CuRiOuS

as a

Cat.

But it's impossible to know
the answers to everything . . .

. . . and sometimes I have
to give my mind a rest.

Sometimes
I feel as

BLIND

as a

Bat.

But when the way
ahead is unclear . . .

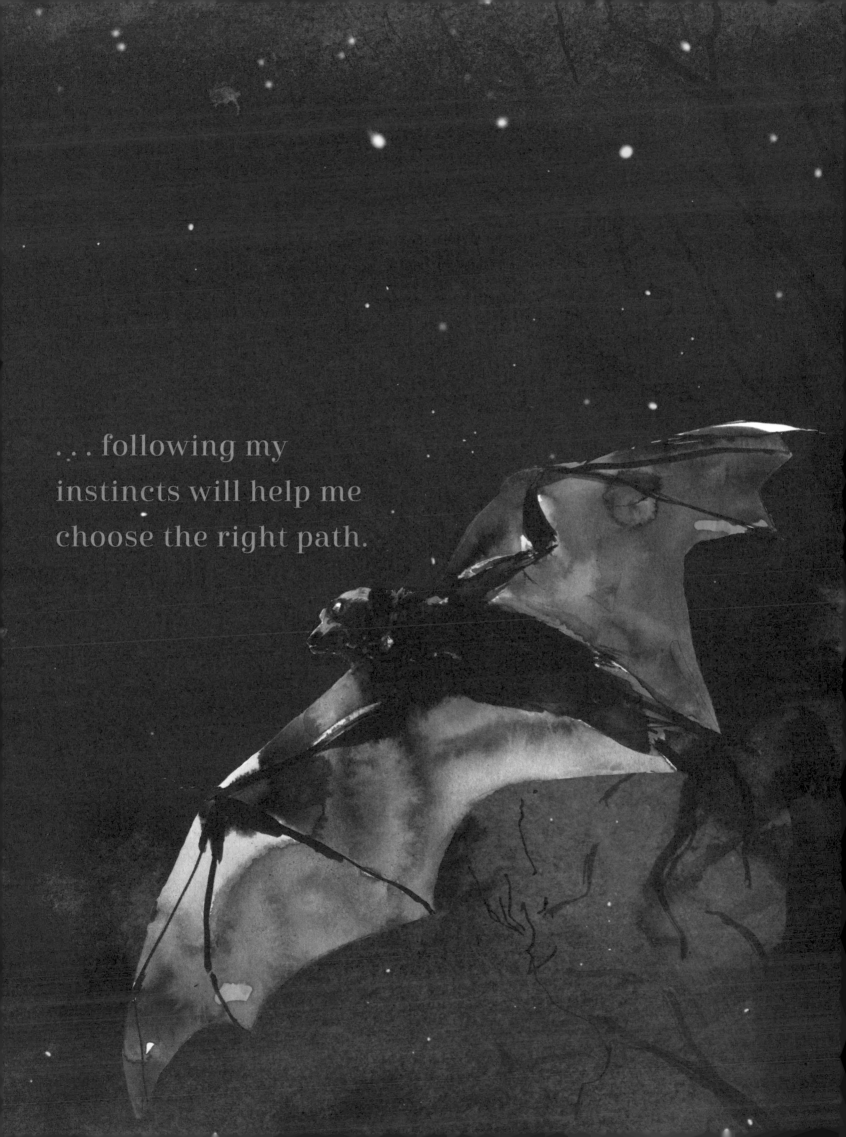

. . . following my
instincts will help me
choose the right path.

Sometimes

I feel as

TIMID

as a

Mouse.

For the gorgeous Daisy and Kirsten Walton – CC
For my lovely daughter, Sophie, who makes me happy – SC

HAPPY!
A RED FOX BOOK 0 09 941364 7

First published in Great Britain by Hutchinson,
an imprint of Random House Children's Books

Hutchinson edition published 2002
Red Fox edition published 2003

1 3 5 7 9 10 8 6 4 2

Text copyright © Caroline Castle, 2002
Illustrations copyright © Sam Childs, 2002

Red Fox Books are published by Random House Children's Books,
61–63 Uxbridge Road, London W5 5SA,
a division of The Random House Group Ltd,
in Australia by Random House Australia (Pty) Ltd,
20 Alfred Street, Milsons Point, Sydney, NSW 2061, Australia,
in New Zealand by Random House New Zealand Ltd,
18 Poland Road, Glenfield, Auckland 10, New Zealand,
and in South Africa by Random House (Pty) Ltd,
Endulini, 5A Jubilee Road, Parktown 2193, South Africa

THE RANDOM HOUSE GROUP Limited Reg. No. 954009
www.kidsatrandomhouse.co.uk

A CIP catalogue record for this book is available from the British Library.

Printed in Hong Kong by Midas Printing Ltd

Happy!

Caroline Castle & Sam Childs

RED FOX

Very early one day Big Zeb got up and smiled a great big smile. 'The sun is up, the sky is blue,' she sang. 'Oh, what a beautiful morning!'

As soon as everyone was awake,
the herd set off for the water hole.
Little Zeb clip-clopped ahead.

'Feeling happy,' he sang.
'Sun up! Sky blue!
Oh, what a beauty!'

As they passed the farmer's garden Big Zeb gasped with delight. 'Oh, look,' she cried, 'all the flowers are blooming.'

Little Zeb did a happy little skip. He was looking forward to seeing his best friend, Little Hippo, who lived in the water hole.

When they arrived, Little Zeb called out, 'Little Hippo! Little Hippo! Sun up! Sky blue! Flowers all blooming. Tip top playing!'

But there was no reply. There was no glub-glub wallowing sound, as there usually was just before Little Hippo poked his head above the water. '*Not* happy,' said Little Zeb.

'Never mind,' said Big Zeb.
'He's sure to be here soon.'

Little Zeb waited

and waited

and waited.

But soon the sun was high in the sky and there was no sign of Little Hippo. 'You'll have to play on your own,' said Big Zeb.

Little Zeb was *not* happy playing on his own. Things were just not the same without Little Hippo. He trotted off into the jungle. 'Sun up! Sky blue!' he sang to try to cheer himself up.

'Oh, what a beauty,' he tried again.
There was a rustling in the bushes,
followed by a great gasp of pleasure.

'Ooo!' cried Little Piggy.
'Who me? Me, a beauty?'

Little Piggy danced around in a circle.
'Me, the beauty,' she sang.
Little Zeb wasn't sure that Little Piggy
was beautiful, but she seemed so
happy, she made Little Zeb
feel more cheerful too.

'Let's wallow!' cried Little Piggy,
and they wallowed.

'Let's jump!' cried Little Piggy,
and they jumped.

'Let's run!' cried Little Piggy,
and they ran...

and they ran
and they ran
and they ran
straight into...

Little Hippo, who had slept too long and had been searching everywhere for Little Zeb.

Little Zeb pushed Little Piggy forward.
'Here's the beauty,' he said proudly,
'our new friend!'

'Let's wallow!' cried Little Piggy,
and they wallowed.

'Let's snuffle!'
cried Little Zeb,
and they snuffled.

Glug!

Big Zeb smiled when she saw the three babies. 'Well, you should be happy now,' she said to Little Zeb, 'now you have *two* friends to play with.'

Little Zeb thought he would burst with joy.
'Sun up! Sky blue!' he cried.

**More Little Zeb picture books
for you to enjoy:**

Gorgeous!

Naughty!

Little Zeb and Friends

Little Zeb's Big Question